GOAL GETTERS
EXPLORING VALUES, FEELINGS, AND GOALS
Grades 4-6

Written by L.M. Conway
Illustrated by Beverly Armstrong

The Learning Works

Edited by Sherri M. Butterfield

The purchase of this book entitles the individual teacher to reproduce copies for use in the classroom.

The reproduction of any part for an entire school or school system or for commercial use is strictly prohibited.

No form of this work may be reproduced or transmitted or recorded without written permission from the publisher.

Copyright © 1984
THE LEARNING WORKS, INC.
P.O. Box 6187
Santa Barbara, CA 93160
All rights reserved.
Printed in the United States of America

Introduction

"Know thyself" read the inscription at the ancient Delphic Oracle; but in this busy modern world, we seldom take time to get acquainted with ourselves, to list our likes and dislikes, to examine our strengths and weaknesses, to be aware of *exactly* who we are and who we'd like to be.

The purpose of **Goal Getters** is to help students come to know themselves, to understand the ways in which they are like other boys and girls their age and to appreciate the ways in which they are different—unique.

This book includes activities that deal with using time, spending money, expressing preferences, solving problems, examining values, setting goals, and organizing time and applying talents to reach the goals that have been set.

Contents

Circles	5
A Few of My Favorite Things	6
On an Island With...	7
If I Had a Million Dollars	8
How Do You Feel About...?	9
What Will They Say About Me?	10
I Would Rather Be	11
Alone on a Raft	12
Which Road Will I Take?	13
Wishing Well	14
The Time of Your Life	15
Turn a Weakness into a Strength	16
Choose Your Horoscope	17
Horoscopes	18-20
What Is Success?	21
Rules for Success	22
A Success Story	23
Things That Bug Me	24
Chart a Solution	25
Everyone Has Highs and Lows	26
Let Off Steam	27
It All Depends on Your Point of View	28
Changing Your Point of View	29
Putting the Pieces Together	30
Help Wanted!	31
Classified Ads	32-33
Program Plan	34
Send Some Good News/Receive Some Good News	35
Characteristics	36
Characteristics a Friend Should Have	37
Characteristics a Father Should Have	38
Characteristics a Mother Should Have	39
Characteristics I Should Have	40
Characteristics I Like Least	41
Don't Wait Too Long!	42
Keep Your Eye on the Target	43
This Month's Goals	44
This Year's Milestones	45
The Ten-Year Race	46
Getting Organized	47
You Are One in a Million!	48

Name _____

Circles

In the circles below, draw as many things as you can think of in five minutes which are often circular in shape. For example, one of your circles might be a button or a wheel. When you have finished, compare your circle drawings with those created by a friend. How many are similar? How many are different? Are more of them alike or different? Why?

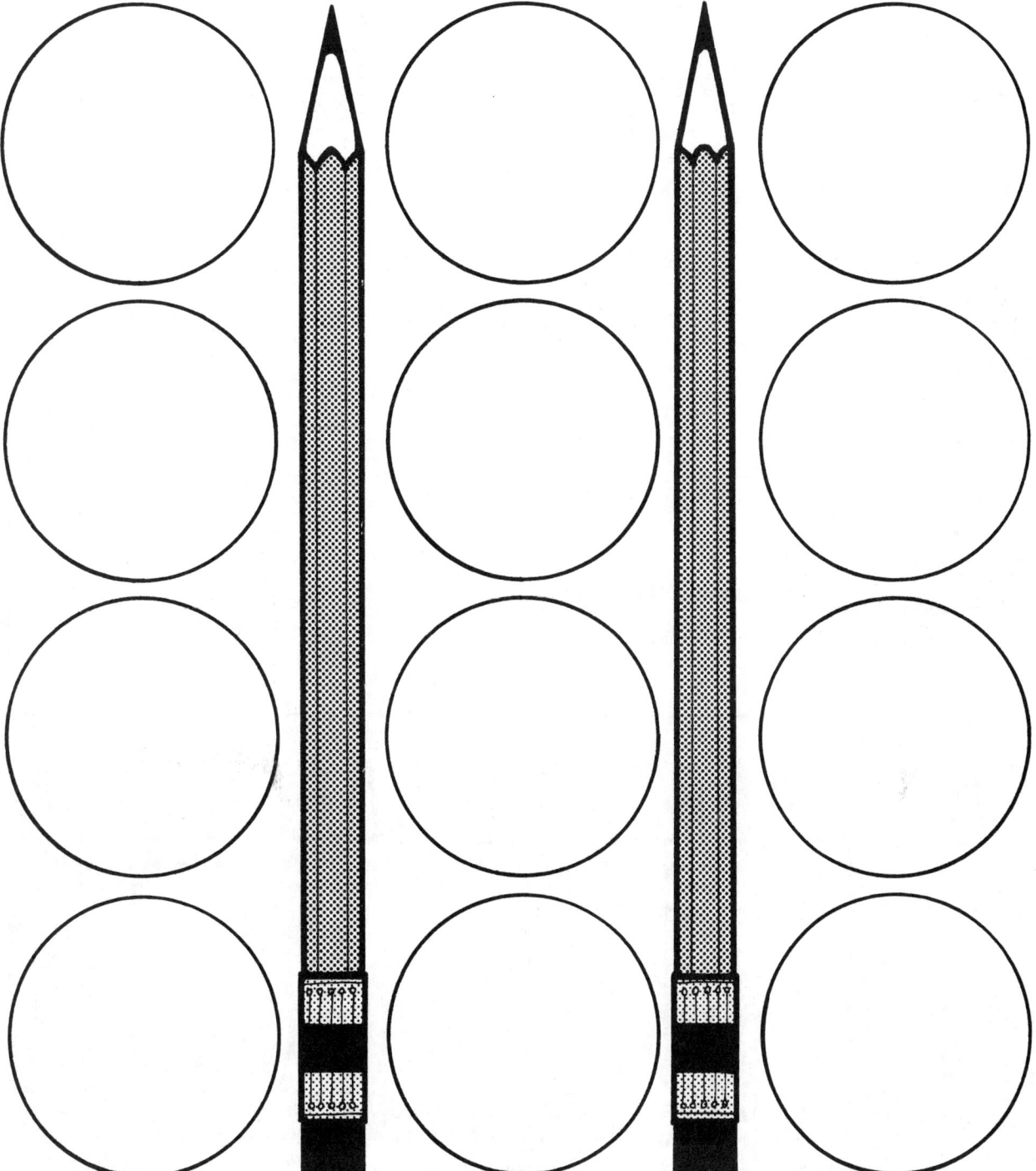

Goal Getters
© 1984 — The Learning Works, Inc.

A Few of My Favorite Things

You know perfectly well which foods you do enjoy eating and which ones you do *not* enjoy eating. You also know your favorite color, form of entertainment, sports, place to visit, season of the year, and thing to do. Just for fun, make a list of your personal favorites. Then, compare your list with one written by a friend. How many of your favorites are the same? How many are different? Why?

color to see	
color to wear	
food to eat	
form of entertainment	
sport to play	
sport to watch	
place to visit	
season of the year	
thing to do	

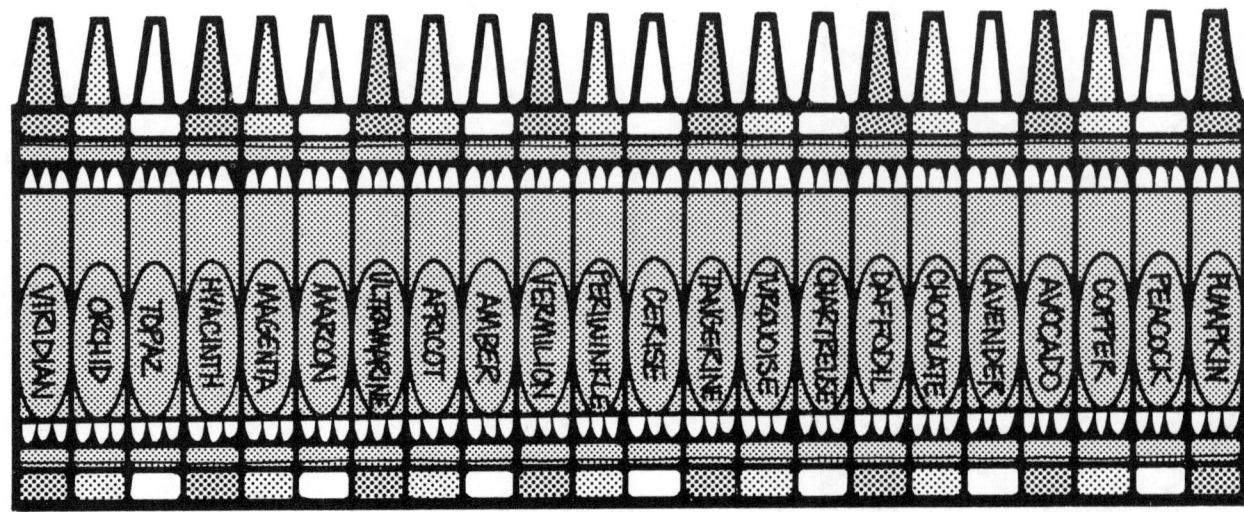

On an Island With…

If you had to spend a year on an island with only one companion, which of the following people would you choose? Name and explain your choice on the lines below.

- a blind doctor
- a clumsy carpenter
- a crazy scientist
- a dishonest lawyer
- a greedy farmer
- a grumpy journalist
- an honest but selfish politician
- an old movie star
- a very silly comedian
- a very talkative salesperson

Name _____

If I Had a Million Dollars

How many times have you longed for a large sum of money? Perhaps you have wished for a hundred, a thousand, or even a million dollars. Do you think that a million dollars would solve your problems or create more problems for you? What would you do with all of that money? First, think about it for a few minutes. Then, on the lines below, list ten things you would buy or do with a million dollars.

1. _____
2. _____
3. _____
4. _____
5. _____
6. _____
7. _____
8. _____
9. _____
10. _____

Name _____

How Do You Feel About…?

How do you feel about the things pictured below? Show your feelings by rating each thing on a scale from one through five, where one means that you don't like it at all, and five means that you like it a lot. For each picture, circle the number that shows how you feel.

1 2 3 4 5	1 2 3 4 5	1 2 3 4 5	1 2 3 4 5
camping tent	snake	can of spinach	book: About a Million Riddles
1 2 3 4 5	1 2 3 4 5	1 2 3 4 5	1 2 3 4 5
car	football	Ferris wheel	handheld video game
1 2 3 4 5	1 2 3 4 5	1 2 3 4 5	1 2 3 4 5
jogger	fight (BAM!)	report card	spider
1 2 3 4 5	1 2 3 4 5	1 2 3 4 5	1 2 3 4 5
banana split	Advanced Mathematics book	rain cloud	electric guitar

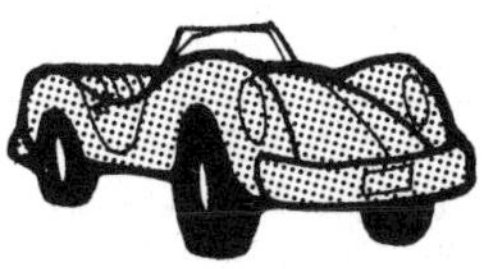

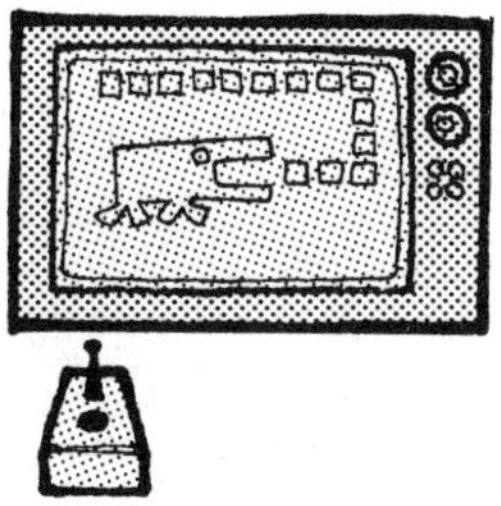

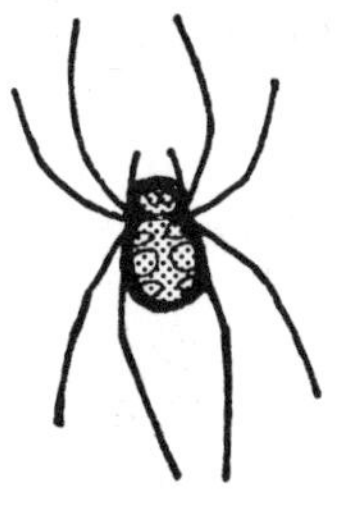

Goal Getters
© 1984 — The Learning Works, Inc.

Name _____

What Will They Say About Me?

Have you ever wondered what people say about you when you're not around to hear? Have you ever thought about what they will say when you're gone? Pretend that you can hear some members of your family or some of your closest friends talking about you when they think that you're not around to listen. On the lines below, write in short play form what two of them might say.

_____
_____
_____
_____
_____
_____
_____

Now think about the way you would like to be thought of after you're gone. On this old tombstone, write an epitaph to help people remember you *exactly* that way.

Goal Getters
© 1984 — The Learning Works, Inc.

Name _____

I Would Rather Be

Have you ever heard someone say, "I would rather be _____"? For each numbered pair below, put an **x** in the right- or left-hand box to show which one you would rather be.

1. ☐ first-string quarterback on the football team — or — ☐ lead guitarist in a band
2. ☐ editor of the school newspaper — or — ☐ star of the school play
3. ☐ head cheerleader — or — ☐ an accomplished pianist
4. ☐ a champion figure skater — or — ☐ a champion roller skater
5. ☐ a gymnast — or — ☐ a soccer star
6. ☐ the heir to a fortune — or — ☐ a genius
7. ☐ an artist who creates beautiful paintings or sculptures — or — ☐ a composer who writes beautiful music
8. ☐ a playwright — or — ☐ an actor or an actress
9. ☐ an author who writes fiction — or — ☐ a journalist who reports facts
10. ☐ the state spelling champion — or — ☐ the state track and field champion
11. ☐ the scientist who finds a cure for a fatal disease — or — ☐ a doctor who successfully treats sick people
12. ☐ a forest ranger who spends much time alone and outside — or — ☐ a criminal lawyer who spends much time with people and in court
13. ☐ a champion skier — or — ☐ a champion surfer
14. ☐ the best student in your school — or — ☐ the most popular student in your school
15. ☐ the best-looking student in your school — or — ☐ the best-liked student in your school
16. ☐ an international sports champion — or — ☐ an international chess champion
17. ☐ an adventurer and world traveler — or — ☐ a person to whom there really is no place like home

Goal Getters
© 1984 — The Learning Works, Inc.

Alone on a Raft

Imagine that you are alone on a raft in the middle of the Pacific Ocean. The raft is riding low in the water, and you must lighten the load. You must throw overboard all of the objects listed below except two. First, choose and underline the two objects that you will keep. Then, on the lines below, explain the reasons for your choices.

- a trunk filled with coins from a sunken ship
- twelve cans of condensed milk
- a fishing pole, fishing tackle, and bait
- a first aid kit
- a shortwave radio with weak batteries
- a life jacket
- a box of flares
- a large container of shark repellent
- a bucket and a rope

Which Road Will I Take?

You are aware of your goals, and you know that you must follow a particular road to reach them; but along that road, there will be obstacles to block your path and easy outs to lead you astray. On the lines below, list some of your goals and some of the things that may prevent you from reaching them.

Goals

_____

_____

_____

_____

_____

_____

Possible Obstacles

_____

_____

_____

_____

Name _____

Wishing Well

If you could wish at the wishing well ten times for anything except money and material possessions and you *knew* that all of your wishes would come true, what ten things would you wish for?

1. _____
2. _____
3. _____
4. _____
5. _____

6. _____
7. _____
8. _____
9. _____
10. _____

Name _____

The Time of Your Life

Pretend that this clock face represents your entire lifetime. If each hour stands for eight years, draw hands on the clock to show how many years of your life have gone by. Then, in one column below, list some of the things you have accomplished in the time that has gone by. In the other column, list some of the things that you hope to accomplish in the time that is yet to come.

My Accomplishments	
Past	Future

Goal Getters
© 1984 — The Learning Works, Inc.

Turn a Weakness into a Strength

History is full of stories about people who overcame handicaps and turned weaknesses of one sort or another into strengths. For example, Demosthenes, the greatest orator in ancient Greece, is said to have had a naturally weak voice and to have stuttered. According to legend, he overcame his stuttering by speaking with pebbles in his mouth, and he strengthened his voice by repeating poetry as he ran uphill and by practicing his speeches near the roaring surf. Ludwig van Beethoven wrote some of his greatest music after he became deaf, Thomas Edison claimed that his deafness enabled him to concentrate better, and neither Winston Churchill nor Albert Einstein always did well in school.

Do you have a weakness that you would like to turn into a strength? In one column below, list some things about yourself that you would like to change. In the other column, list some ways in which you might go about changing these things. If you need more space, continue your list on another sheet of paper.

Things I Would Like to Change	Ways I Could Change These Things

Name _____

Choose Your Horoscope

A horoscope is a description of one's personality and/or a forecast of one's future based on the relative positions of the planets and constellations, or signs of the zodiac, at a specific time. Horoscopes are published daily in some newspapers and are read by many people. First, read the sample horoscopes on pages 18, 19, and 20. Then, choose the one that fits you best. Write the title for the horoscope you chose on this line.

_____

If none of the horoscopes suits you, write your own horoscope on the lines below. In doing so, you may wish to combine parts from the horoscopes on the following pages or from other horoscopes you have read.

_____
_____
_____
_____
_____

Finally, compare your horoscope with those chosen and written by other members of your class. Which horoscope was most popular? Which horoscope was least popular? Why?

Name _____

Horoscopes

1. ARIES (The Ram)

The Intellect

Your intellect enables you to grasp things easily. You also have a strong will and choose your own friends, a few close ones rather than many. You enjoy the good things in life but appreciate simplicity. You like to dig and probe and have a strong desire to succeed. You have the ability to do well in any field you choose.

2. TAURUS (The Bull)

The Traveler

You enjoy change, traveling, meeting different people, and adventure. You do not like to be alone, but neither do you favor strong ties. Because you are somewhat self-centered, you tend to withdraw at times. You like the use of money and tend to overspend. You desire work in the theater, fine arts, or related areas.

3. GEMINI (The Twins)

The Humanitarian

A great love and concern for all mankind singles you out as an outstanding person. You would like to see a better world with less poverty, disease, and suffering. You are concerned about the environment and pollution. You also have many good friends who respect your ideals. It would be natural for you to choose work in the social sciences, medicine, teaching, environmental sciences, or the Peace Corps.

4. CANCER (The Crab)

The Sport

You are an active, energetic, highly competitive person. Sports, games, and contests are of special interest to you. You pay close attention to the workings of your body and use exercise and nutrition to maintain good health. You may never be a professional athlete, but you will always be interested in sports and will continue to pursue them for recreation throughout your life.

Horoscopes
(continued)

The Business Person

Business, corporations, and finances bring out the best in you. You are efficient and prompt; and you like for everything to be clean, neat, orderly, and modern. Your friends might classify you as a workaholic. You are likely to know *exactly* how much money you have at any moment down to the last cent. A strong character and self-discipline keep your emotions in check at all times.

5. LEO
(The Lion)

6. VIRGO
(The Virgin)

The Nature Lover

You love the outdoors and nature. Peace and quiet dominate your life. You value the time you spend in quiet meditation. You are not motivated by money or by material possessions. You are kind to all living things and respect the laws of nature. Farming, forestry, or the great outdoors will probably claim your talents.

7. LIBRA
(The Balance)

The Legal Mind

There is no stopping you when you are pursuing what you believe is right. Justice, government, and politics consume your energies. You treat others fairly and insist upon the same treatment in return. Your wise leadership has the support of many. Your future lies in government, law, law enforcement, politics, or a related field.

8. SCORPIO
(The Scorpion)

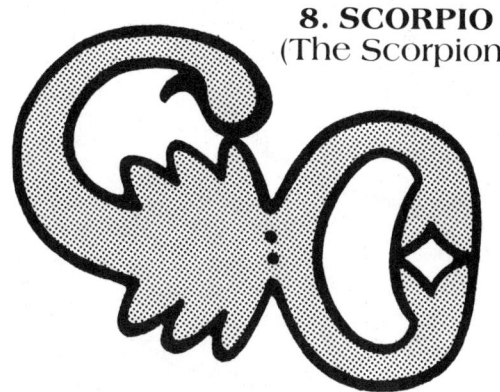

The Creative Person

You like to make things with your hands. You are creative and original in your work, hobbies, and the atmosphere in which you live. Cooking, crafts, mechanics, carpentry, and/or do-it-yourself projects fill your time. You enjoy company, but you can also entertain yourself easily when you are alone. A career in carpentry, construction, engineering, homemaking, or mechanics will appeal to you.

Horoscopes
(continued)

9. SAGITTARIUS
(The Archer)

The Philanthropist

You truly love the fine arts. If you become wealthy, you will be a patron of art, music, sculpture, or theater. Fine food and travel also beckon to you. Sentimentality and honor are your strongest traits, but you are known to prize material possessions of great value. You should seek work in the fine arts, the theater, or some related area.

10. CAPRICORN
(The Goat)

The Socialite

People are drawn to you and confide in you. You are outgoing and enjoy social gatherings of all kinds and the company of many friends. You enjoy the good things in life as well as the simple things. You like work in which you are involved with interesting people. Your future lies in any one of many areas in which you can have much social interaction.

11. AQUARIUS
(The Water Bearer)

The Scientist

Medicine, teaching, and research are your interests. You have few friends, but they are very good ones. Most people and things do not impress you. Because of this fact, your thinking is not easily influenced. You like facts. Although you are independent and prefer to work alone, you are sometimes lonely.

12. PISCES
(The Fishes)

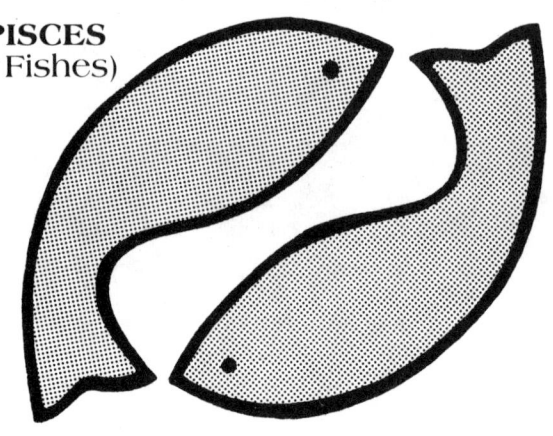

The Artist

Beauty, color, art, flowers, and antiques are some of your favorite things. You are old-fashioned and sentimental, a person with inner fires and desires. You seek love and attachments because you enjoy both giving and receiving. Decorating, painting, and selling fine furniture and art appeal to you.

Name _____

What Is Success?

People have very different ideas about what success is. They may see it as excellence, fame, happiness, recognized achievement, satisfaction, wealth, or some combination of these elements. On the lines below, write a paragraph in which you explain what success means to you.

Rules for Success

1. Be honest.
2. Always work hard.
3. Never give up.
4. Be kind to everyone.
5. Be thrifty.

Listed above are five rules for success. Read them carefully, and then make your own list of ten rules. You may include any or all of the rules already listed if you agree that they are important to follow in your personal search for success.

1. _____
2. _____
3. _____
4. _____
5. _____
6. _____
7. _____
8. _____
9. _____
10. _____

Name _____

A Success Story

Usually, successful people have worked very hard to achieve their success, and people who are most loved have been most generous in giving love to others. First, think of someone you know who is successful or who is loved and appreciated. Then, think about why this is so. Record your thoughts on the lines below.

_____
_____
_____
_____
_____
_____
_____
_____

Name _____

Things That Bug Me

From time to time, everyone is annoyed by certain people, situations, or things. Often, the annoyance is increased by the time spent brooding over it. Don't waste time sulking over the insignificant. On the lines below, list ten things that annoy you most. Then, consider carefully whether they are worth the time you spend fretting over them or might just as easily be forgotten or ignored.

1. _____
2. _____
3. _____
4. _____
5. _____
6. _____
7. _____
8. _____
9. _____
10. _____

Chart a Solution

Some everyday problems cannot be ignored. They need to be faced and solved. One way to solve problems is by thinking about them in an organized manner. To do so, follow these simple steps.

1. Start.
2. Write a brief description of your problem.
3. Write down all of the solutions you can think of.
4. Consider these solutions carefully, and choose one.
5. Put the solution you have chosen into effect. Try it!
6. Evaluate the problem. Has it been solved by the solution you tried?
7. If so, you have been successful. If not, return to step 4, select another possible solution, and try it.

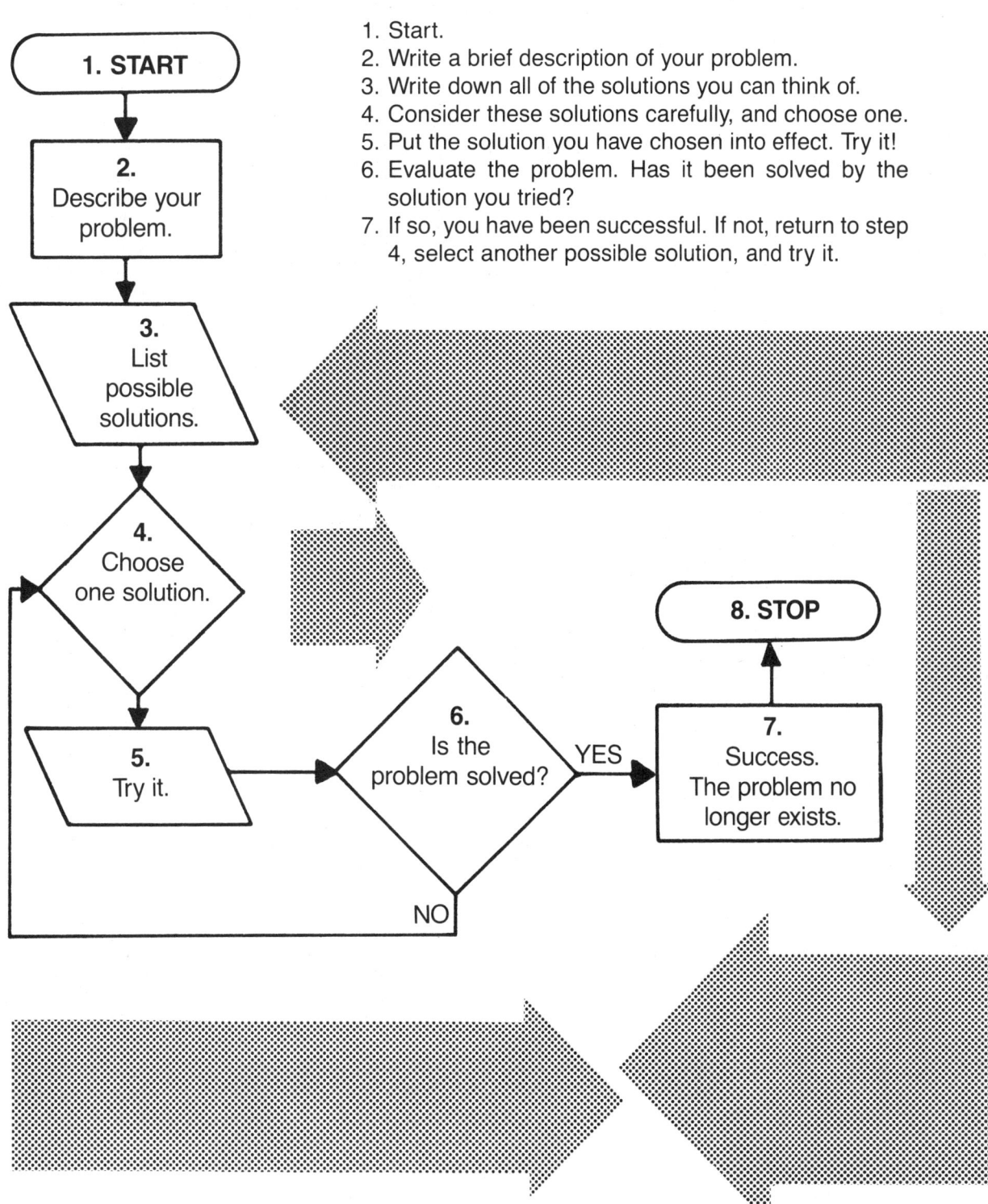

Everyone Has Highs and Lows

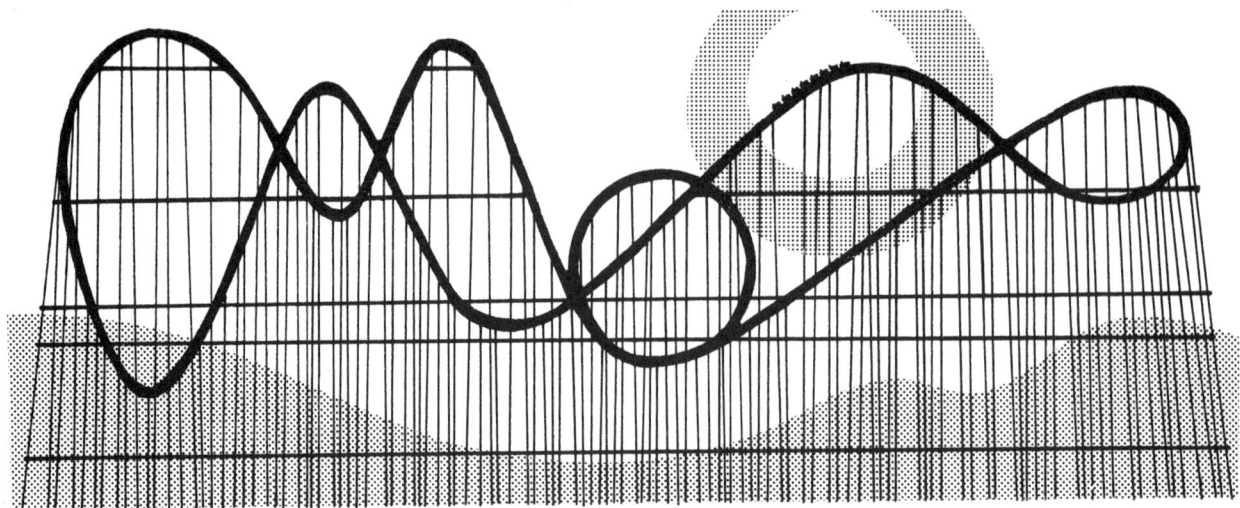

Everyone feels low in spirits, or depressed, at one time or another. When things hit bottom, it's okay to feel bad; but it's not okay to act angry at everyone around you or to continue to feel bad for a long, long time. Remember, there'll be plenty of hills and thrills ahead if you are ready for them. In the list below, underline the things that have caused the lowest lows on your roller coaster of life. Then add your own highs and lows to the list.

1. getting a bad grade on a test that you studied for
2. not having enough money to do something you *really* wanted to do or to buy something you *really* wanted to buy
3. losing a game or contest of some sort
4. having a complexion that's not clear
5. having a family pet die
6. watching a friend move away
7. having family problems you can't solve
8. being misunderstood when your intentions were good
9. not looking as pretty or as handsome as you would like to look
10. not being as talented or as capable in some area as you would like to be

Highs	
Lows	

Name _____

Let Off Steam

When your roller coaster is down, it's time to let off steam. Here are eight suggestions. Read them, and then add two more to the list.

1. Have a good cry, but then go on to other things.

2. Talk to a friend.

3. Get physical. Jog, swim, or play a game of some kind.

4. Tackle a task that you have been putting off. Do something productive that will bring you a sense of accomplishment.

5. Treat yourself to a pleasant experience. Do something you enjoy. Bake cookies, read a book, or listen to music.

6. Express your feelings. Write a poem or story about them.

7. Be creative. Draw, paint, sculpt, or design something.

8. Think about happier times and past successes.

9. _____

10. _____

It All Depends on Your Point of View

To a farmer, growing vegetables may be hard work.

To a businessman, growing vegetables may be a pleasure.

Name _____

Changing Your Point of View

At one time or another, almost all of us must do things that we do not enjoy doing. Often, we can make unpleasant tasks more enjoyable simply by changing our attitude, or point of view, about them. In the space below, draw a picture of yourself doing something that you don't like to do. Then, on the lines below the picture, list five things that you could do to make this task more pleasant. The next time you must do this task, put some of your good ideas into action.

1. _____
2. _____
3. _____
4. _____
5. _____

Name _____

Putting the Pieces Together

"He's going to pieces." "Get yourself together." These are two common expressions which tell us that we do not always act as whole persons. We do not always use all of our talents and abilities in a balanced fashion. Sometimes, we forget about, or neglect, important parts of ourselves. Label the puzzle pieces pictured below to indicate parts of your personality. Be careful not to forget any!

Name _____

Help Wanted!

Look over the classified ads on pages 32 and 33. See which ones would interest you most if you were looking for a job. Circle the ones you would like to investigate.

Name _____

Classified Ads

BOOKKEEPER
For a toy manufacturer. Experience preferred but not necessary. Job includes keeping track of parts purchases, logging orders, and handling payroll. Good salary and fringe benefits. Call 222-1268.

CABINETMAKER
To do rough and finish work. Experience preferred. Will consider inexperienced hard worker with good references. Call Classy Cabinets at 227-1948.

CONSTRUCTION—$7/HR.
Many openings.   Start now.
NAIL DRIVERS—$3 TO $5/HR.
Need now.   Easy hours!
Call 221-1111

COOK/EXPERIENCED
Breakfast and lunch chef in hotel coffee shop. 6 a.m. to 2 p.m. five days. Salary negotiable. Must have own reliable transportation and good references. Call Mrs. Johnson at 224-1211 before 3 p.m.

DENTAL ASSISTANT
Personable assistant needed for busy dentist's office. Must have a minimum of one year of chairside experience. Call 228-1649, and ask for Dr. Ache.

EXECUTIVE SECRETARY
Typing, office skills, with several years of experience in executive field. Applicant must have a pleasing telephone voice and be able to double as receptionist. No shorthand necessary. Call 276-8420, and ask for Ima Typest.

DRIVER WANTED
Must be at least 25 years old and have a valid state driver's license. Contact Itch N. Togo at 261-6181.

CLASS A MECHANIC
For heavy-duty truck and diesel units. Must be able to work independently and to troubleshoot big rigs. Excellent starting salary and employee benefits. Call 221-6066 between 8 a.m. and 5:30 p.m., and ask for Joe.

MECHANICS
Needed to do maintenance and repair at major auto assembly plant. Top pay, excellent benefits, profit sharing, modern facilities. Phone 222-5558.

MEDICAL TECHNOLOGIST
Physicians' office in northwest part of city seeks registered medical technologist to work from 8:30 a.m. to 5:30 p.m., five days a week. Experience required. Call Dr. I. M. Smart at 221-9991.

NURSING ASSISTANTS
Nursing home, all shifts. Contact Imogene Sims at 224-6789 between 8 and 4 on Monday through Friday.

OFFICE WORK. Varied duties. Must be able to type and use a word processor. Top pay for right person. Call 223-3394.

PERSONNEL COUNSELOR
Applicant must be able to interview, hire, train, supervise, and dismiss employees at large department store. Experience preferred, but will train sharp, mature person. "People" or sales experience helpful. If interested, call 223-6616.

PHYSICAL THERAPIST
Needed immediately for an accredited hospital and nursing home. Must be experienced and currently licensed in this state. Excellent benefits and starting salary along with a promising future. Call 222-4545 collect.

PHYSICAL THERAPY ASSISTANT
Opportunity to work with both orthopedic and rehabilitation patients. State license required. Call 223-6996, and ask for Beverly.

Name _____

Classified Ads
(continued)

PIPELINE CONSTRUCTION
Need experienced foreman, backhoe operator, and pipe layer. Must have at least two years of experience with large water and sewer installation. Call
PRO PIPE LAYERS
220-4281

PLANT ENGINEER
Individual with related engineering degree. Experienced in plant or building maintenance for multiplant operations. This leading manufacturer of menswear offers excellent salary, fringe benefits, and working conditions. Submit complete resume of education, experience, and salary requirements to
FAMOUS MAKER MENSWEAR
4750 Cotton Street   Mobile, Alabama

PIANO player wanted for Gospel group, the Calvaryman Quartet. Call 221-1221 between 6 p.m. and 11 p.m.

PICTURE FRAMING
Would you like to work in a shop where quality, not profit, is the prime consideration? Experience preferred but not necessary. Apply in person at
THE FRAME GAME

PILOT-Photographer. Aerial mapping. Five years of experience. Own plane a plus but not a must. Call
FLY-FOTO (359-3686)

PLANT HELP
SECOND SHIFT
LAYOUT PERSON
WELDERS
Call 224-4444

RECEPTIONIST
Doctor's office. Must be able to greet patients on the telephone and in person, schedule appointments, perform general clerical tasks, and act as insurance clerk. Must type. Write P.O. Box 999, Atlanta, Georgia.

EXECUTIVE SECRETARY TO PRESIDENT
Experienced executive secretary for well-located office. Must be attractive, have good personality, and be extremely skilled at typing, filing, and letter composition. Send resume and work sample to   Zeck Q. Tive
P.O. Box 6730 Terminal Station
Los Angeles, California

TRAVEL. Wholesale Travel Company is looking for individual to sell tours. Salary plus commission. Some hotel and ticket discounts. Call 220-1111.

TRUCK DRIVER. City experienced, Class 1 license. Polygraph required. Call between 10 a.m. and noon. 224-6400.

TV TECHNICIAN
We need one super TV technician. Will pay top salary to right person. Call Rich TV for an interview.

WAREHOUSE CLERK
Order pulling, shipping, and receiving. Many company benefits. Advance Process Company, 220-0339.

WAITRESSES/WAITERS wanted for the Make-Mine-Bar-B-Q restaurant chain. Apply in person only to corporate offices in El Paso, Texas.

WANTED
NAIL DRIVERS and carpenters. Experienced only. Apply in person to construction site at
222 East Main

DOCTOR NEEDED for small practice on secluded island off the coast of Georgia. Population 2,000. Financial reward small. Satisfaction and appreciation large. Call 222-1022.

PROGRAMMER
Progressive brokerage firm requires programmer experienced with tandem non-stop system and COBOL. Accounting background a plus. Negotiable, competitive salary and above-average benefits. Qualified applicants send resume to
Computer Department
P.O. Box 1372
Santa Monica, California

PROGRAMMING SOFTWARE SPECIALIST
Well-established small company has immediate need for software engineers experienced in compiler development, real-time operating systems, and configuration management. Excellent benefits include profit sharing. Please send resume to
SPECIALIZED SOFTWARE SYSTEMS
1010 Wilshire Blvd.
Beverly Hills, California

ENGINEERING PROGRAMMER/ ANALYST
Engineering firm with long-term defense contract needs programmer with thorough working knowledge of electro-optical systems and ability to program in both FORTRAN and Pascal. Degree in electrical engineering a must. Advanced degree a plus. Duties include image enhancement, systems analysis, and encounter simulation. Qualified engineers send resume to P.O. Box 610, Irvine, California.

PRODUCTION SUPERVISOR
Specialty manufacturer seeks a person with leadership capabilities. Position requires mechanical/shop experience and the ability to read blueprints, micrometers, and calipers. Must be able to read and speak English with ease. Good company benefits. Call 516-9099 between 8 a.m. and 5 p.m.
Equal Opportunity Employer

ELECTRONIC TECHNICIAN
Work as field service technician in the Los Angeles area for a firm servicing computer systems. Must have three to five years of experience with hard disk minicomputer systems. Printer experience is required. Send resume to
Field Service Department
5 Mockingbird Lane
Huntington Beach, California

FITNESS COACH
Exclusive membership gym seeks qualified fitness coach to design and supervise exercise programs for adults. Position requires experience in the use of both Nautilus and Universal equipment. Healthy appearance is a must. Apply in person between 9 a.m. and 5 p.m. to
Fitness 4 U

MURAL ARTIST
Talented artist needed to help busy interior designer create custom environments for discerning clients. Call 837-2040 to make appointment for portfolio showing.

ACTORS/ACTRESSES
Urgently needed for parts in a musical production at a local dinner theater. If interested, please send photo and summary of professional credits to P.O. Box 60, Martha's Vineyard, Massachusetts.

Name _____

Program Plan

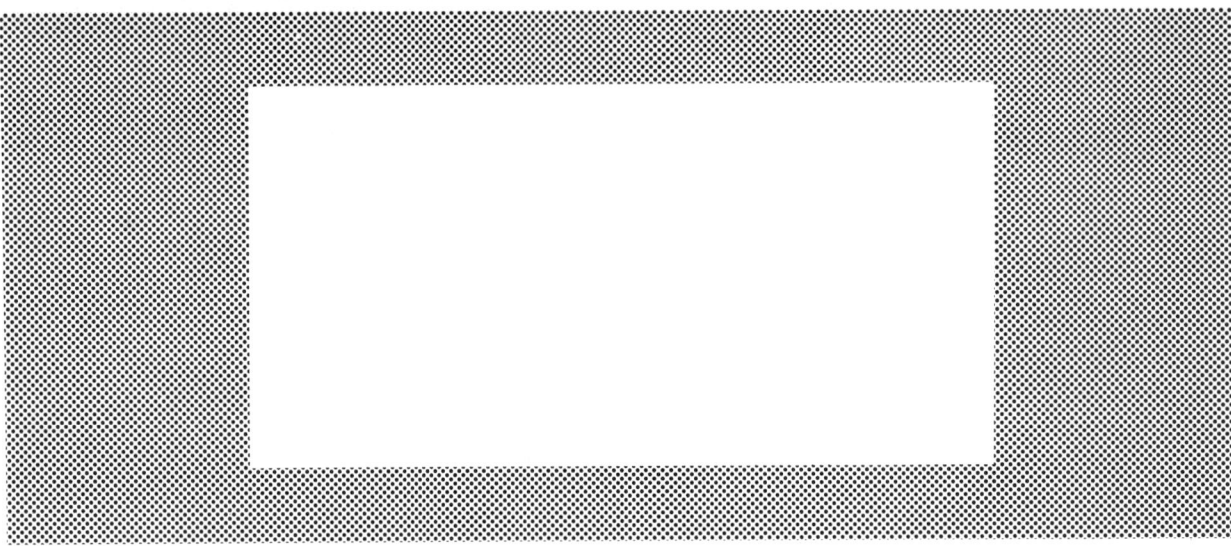

Choose an ad from the ones on pages 32 and 33 or find one in your local newspaper. Cut it out and paste it in the box above. On the lines below, list the specific educational, skill, and experience requirements needed to fill the position described in the ad. Then, in the spaces provided, explain what *you* would do to fulfill each requirement.

Requirements	Means of Fulfilling Requirements

Name _____

Send Some Good News

Everyone likes to receive good news. Pick any person you know, and write a good-news telegram to him or her. Because this is a make-believe exercise, stretch your imagination. Because words in a telegram cost money, keep your message brief.

TELEGRAM

TO: _____

_____

_____

_____

_____

FROM: _____

Receive Some Good News

Now write a make-believe telegram to yourself. Include some news you would *really* like to receive.

TELEGRAM

TO: _____

_____

_____

_____

_____

FROM: _____

Characteristics

Characteristics are the special qualities of personality and appearance that make one person different from others. Below is a list of some of the characteristics that are often used to describe people. First, read this list carefully. Then, use it to do the activities on pages 37, 38, 39, and 40.

ambition	enthusiasm	patience
attractiveness	fairness	politeness
beauty	gentleness	popularity
bravery	grace	punctuality
cleanliness	graciousness	sensitivity
cleverness	happiness	seriousness
consideration	helpfulness	strength
courage	honesty	strong-mindedness
creativity	humility	talent
culture	intelligence	thoughtfulness
dedication	kindness	thrift
dependability	loyalty	truthfulness
discipline	neatness	understanding
education	organization	wealth
energy	originality	wit

Goal Getters
© 1984 — The Learning Works, Inc.

Name _____

Characteristics a Friend Should Have

Look at the list of characteristics on page 36. Decide which ten of these characteristics you would like for your best friend to have. If your best friend is a boy, write the characteristics you have chosen on the sign held by the boy. If your best friend is a girl, write them on the sign held by the girl.

Characteristics a Father Should Have

Look at the list of characteristics on page 36. Decide which ten of these characteristics a father should have. Write the ten characteristics you have chosen on the lines below.

Name _____

Characteristics a Mother Should Have

Look at the list of characteristics on page 36. Decide which ten of these characteristics a mother should have. Write the ten characteristics you have chosen on the lines below.

Name _____

Characteristics I Should Have

Look at the list of characteristics on page 36. Decide which ten of these characteristics you should have. If you are a boy, write the characteristics you have chosen on the sign held by the boy. If you are a girl, write the characteristics you have chosen on the sign held by the girl.

Name _____

Characteristics I Like Least

While there are some characteristics we want or expect the people in our life to have, there are other characteristics we wish no one had. From the characteristics listed here, select the six you like the *least*, and write them on the numbered lines. Then, in the space below, draw a picture of a person who has at least three of these characteristics.

cowardice	loudness	sloppiness
criticalness	messiness	stubbornness
deceitfulness	moodiness	stupidity
dishonesty	obstinacy	sulkiness
dullness	quietness	timidity
fearfulness	rudeness	ugliness
immorality	sarcasticness	unhappiness
impatience	self-centeredness	unkindness
inflexibility	selfishness	untidiness
jealousy	shyness	verbosity
laziness	skepticism	weakness

1. _____   4. _____

2. _____   5. _____

3. _____   6. _____

Goal Getters
© 1984 — The Learning Works, Inc.

Don't Wait Too Long!

Once you have decided that there are some things about yourself which you would like to change, don't wait too long! While you are waiting, your coach may turn into a pumpkin, and you may miss some golden opportunities because you aren't prepared. Instead, get started! In one column below, list some changes that you want to make in your appearance, your habits, or your goals. In the other column, list some steps *you* can take to make these changes. Then, take the first step today!

Changes I Want to Make	Steps I Can Take to Make These Changes
	1.
	2.
	3.
	1.
	2.
	3.

Keep Your Eye on the Target

In archery, you are more likely to hit the bull's-eye if you keep your eye on the target. To reach a goal, you must know where you are going and aim yourself in that direction. In the spaces on this target, write some personal goals for this week. Will you keep your desk neater, do *all* of your homework, find time to practice, or clean up your bedroom? Once you have decided on your goals, don't lose sight of them. *Keep your eye on the target!* At the end of the week, check to see how well you have done. Give yourself ten points for each goal you have achieved. Write your total number of points for the week in the bull's-eye.

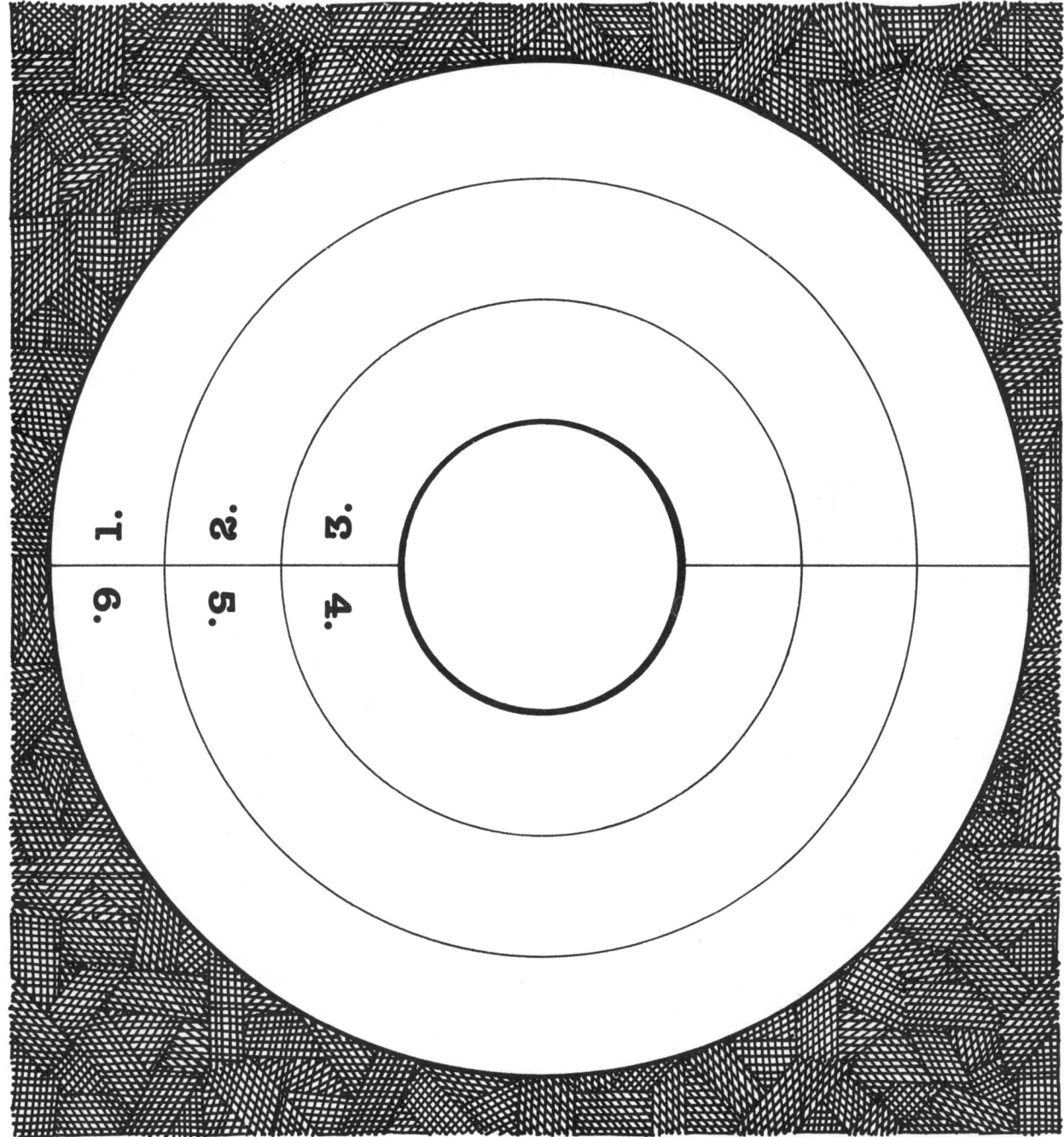

Name _____

This Month's Goals

Some things can be done quickly. Other things take longer to accomplish. To get where you want to go, you'll need to set some short-range goals—things that you can accomplish relatively quickly—and some long-range goals—things that will take longer to accomplish but are important enough to be worth the extra time they take.

On the lines below, list the goals that you plan to achieve this month. At the end of the month, check to see how well you have done. Give yourself ten points for each goal you have reached. Write your total number of points for the month in the score box at the bottom of this page.

1. _____
2. _____
3. _____
4. _____
5. _____
6. _____
7. _____
8. _____
9. _____
10. _____

Goal Getters
© 1984 — The Learning Works, Inc.

This Year's Milestones

Many years ago, distances between towns were marked by stones set beside the road. Thus, these stones—called milestones—were indications of a traveler's progress. Later, the meaning of the word milestone was generalized to mean "a significant point in any journey or development."

What might be some of the significant points along the path from where you are now to where you hope to be in one year? Record them on the lines beside the monthly milestones pictured here.

Goal Getters
© 1984 — The Learning Works, Inc.

Name _____

The Ten-Year Race

Where do you want to be ten years from today? What do you hope to be doing? On the lines below, list or describe some of the goals you have for a decade from now.

Name _____

Getting Organized

To reach your goals for a week, a month, a year, a decade, or a lifetime, you'll need to get organized *today*. Use the first chart below to organize your tasks. Write down school assignments and/or home responsibilities when they are assigned, and then check them off when you complete them. Use the second chart to help you keep track of your after-school time and use it wisely.

Day or Week:

Subject	Assignment or Responsibility	When Due	✔

Week:

Time	Monday	Tuesday	Wednesday	Thursday	Friday
2:00 to 3:00					
3:00 to 4:00					
4:00 to 5:00					
5:00 to 6:00					
6:00 to 7:00					
7:00 to 8:00					
8:00 to 9:00					

Name _____

You Are One in a Million!

No one else looks *exactly* like you look, and no one else does things *exactly* like you do them, because no one else is *exactly* like you. You are one in a million!

What You Need
- one sheet of unlined paper
- pencil
- ruler or straight edge
- scissors
- colored pencils, crayons, or felt-tipped marking pens

What You Do

1. Take a sheet of unlined paper, and fold it in half lengthwise.

2. With a pencil and ruler, draw a line one inch above the fold.

3. Using a pencil, write your first name in cursive along the line. Make the letters as large as possible.

4. With scissors, cut around the *top* of your name, being careful *not* to cut through the fold except at the beginning and at the end.

5. Unfold your name, and turn it so that the first letter is at the top.

6. Make this shape into a creature by adding facial and other features.

7. Use colored pencils, crayons, or felt-tipped marking pens to color your creature.

8. Display your unique creature where you and your friends can see and enjoy it.

Goal Getters
© 1984 — The Learning Works, Inc.